Outside Opportunity's Gate

机会的门外

By *Snow Ray*

Outside Opportunity's Gate
机会的门外

Snow Ray Short Story Collection

瑞雪中英双语小说集

Published by [Majestic River Publisher, LLC] [Hooksett, USA]

ISBN: 979-8-9878406-3-4

Dedication

For those who lost their voices,
but not their light.

献给失去声音，
却从未失去光芒的人们。

Contents　　　目录

6

Outside Opportunity's Gate

Introduction

In these stories, memory and history intertwine with love, resilience, and the quiet struggle for survival.

From university campuses shadowed by political storms to families weighed down by duty and silence, each tale reveals how private lives were bound—and often broken—by the tides of their time.

Written in both Chinese and English, Snow Ray's collection bridges cultures while preserving the tenderness of personal memory and the weight of collective history. These short stories illuminate:

The fragility and endurance of love under pressure,

The cost of silence and sacrifice in ordinary lives,

The courage to step beyond one's circle and seek renewal.

机会的门外

简介

在这些故事中，记忆与历史交织，映照出爱、坚韧与沉默生存的力量。从笼罩左倾政治阴影的校园，到一些不公平的政策，再到被责任与沉默压抑的家庭，每一个故事都揭示了个体生命如何被时代裹挟、甚至撕裂。

Preface

This collection of stories is not about legends, but about ordinary people living through extraordinary times.

They were meant to soar like young birds, yet again and again, fate's unseen hand pushed them away, leaving them stranded outside the gate of opportunity.

Li Jian — a gifted young man, shut out from the university by a single line on a medical report, spent his life with only his accordion as companion.

Fang Ming — a young teacher with grand ambitions, torn between a marriage of duty and a forbidden love, eventually crushed beneath public scorn and social convention.

Professor Lin — who lived through political upheavals, family burdens, and decades of silent endurance, only to find, in his later years, a long-delayed freedom to step "out of the circle."

Their stories are not merely personal tragedies; they are the echoes of an era. Love, marriage, ideals, responsibility—all were reshaped, bruised, or destroyed beneath the heavy stone of history and society.

This collection is not written to mourn their failures, but to preserve their struggles. For it is precisely these flickers of human resilience, hidden in the shadows, that form the truest chorus of a generation.

总序 · 机会的门外

这一组小说，写的不是传奇，而是真实年代里最普通的人。

他们本该像年轻的鸟儿一样振翅高飞，却一次次被命运的风浪裹挟，被无形的手推离机会的门槛之外。

李建—才华横溢的少年，被体检的判语关在了大学门外，一生与手风琴为伴。

方明—满怀抱负的青年教师，在责任婚姻与炽热爱情之间撕裂，最终跌入世俗与舆论的深渊。

林教授—亲历时代起伏，从家庭、事业、责任中挣扎出圈，直到晚年才终于找到走向自然与自由的道路。

他们的故事，既是个人的悲欢，也是一个时代的注脚。爱情、婚姻、理想、责任—

在社会与历史的巨石下，被不断碾压、重塑，留下悲剧，也留下坚韧。

这些故事不是要讲述他们的失败，而是要铭记他们的努力与挣扎。因为正是这些被遮蔽的生命之光，构成了一代人的真实合唱。

Prologue

The circle

To live is to move within it, to be bound by duty, expectation, and the silent weight of tradition.

But when the circle closes too tightly, when breath and choice are pressed away, is there a way out?

And if one does step beyond—does it mean escape, or simply another kind of return?

(1)

The first thing Professor Lin did after retirement was to leave every work group and social circle. For decades, he had never lacked connections, always circulating among meetings, banquets, and collaborations. Yet deep inside, he had long grown weary of such forced liveliness.

He was a man of strong opinions, bold in youth to voice his own thoughts. But in real life, he had been forced again and again to compromise.
From studies to work, from family to duty, his life had always been pushed forward by an invisible hand.

Now, at last, retirement had come. He wanted to shed it all and turn to nature.

(2)

His wife had passed away two years earlier due to chronic illness. The marriage had not been built on love; the couple lacked real depth in their exchanges. Yet over decades, they had treated each other with respect, raising a family together—enough to be called complete.

In youth, he had known a searing love. But as an only son, he bore the burden of "continuing the family line," forced to accept his parents' arrangement. His life resembled the elder brother in Ba Jin's novel Family: personal will pressed down by clan and era, the fire in his heart quietly extinguished.

Still, his career had brought modest success, earning respect from colleagues and society. His child was grown, with a family of his own. The "mission" was complete. So, he told himself:
—It was time to step out of the circle and live as he wished.

(3)

Yet in his heart, one shadow remained. It came from his son's childhood. The first child had been a daughter. But society and family said: "A daughter doesn't count. The Lin family still needs a son."

During the harshest years of the one-child policy, another child meant breaking the law: job loss, crushing fines, even family ruin. He did not want more children, but his wife insisted, and his parents pressed him.

When she became pregnant again, he hesitated. Then he thought:
The child is innocent. Abortion is too cruel. And so, the second child was born in secret.

They dared not register him. He was raised by relatives, calling them "uncle" and "aunt," known to outsiders as a cousin's son from overseas. Only at seven, after countless favors and pleading, did the grandparents secure a household registration, allowing him to return and go to school with his real parents.

But the secret cut like a scar into the boy's heart. Years of distance made him withdrawn and sensitive, burdened with the pain of never daring to call his true parents by name. Professor Lin felt deep guilt, pouring all his care into the boy's education, desperate to make up for what had been lost.

Fortunately, the son grew polite and bright, entered a good university, and later built his own family and career. Over and over, Lin told himself: *It was time to let go.*

(4)

In retirement, he turned toward nature. Mountains, rivers, and wilderness became his new classroom. Birds replaced noise, and the wind thinned the clamor of the world.

To step out was not to discard the past, but to set it down. He had to relearn how to live— for himself alone. Yet in quiet journeys, he often heard echoes between the wind and the trees. Those people, those stories, those friends once beside him but long lost to time.

And then he understood: True freedom was not to escape, but the moment he would one day carry those voices with him—and return.

出圈

序

圈子

活着，就是在圈子里打转，被责任、期待与传统无声的重量所束缚。然而，当圈子收得过紧，当呼吸与选择都被挤压殆尽，还能找到出口吗？而若真的踏出这道圈子——那意味着逃离，还是另一种归来？

(1)

林教授退休后的第一件事，就是退出了所有工作群与朋友圈。

几十年来，他从不缺少人脉，也习惯在各种会议、聚餐与合作里周旋。可在心底，他早已厌倦了这种被迫的热闹。

他曾经是一个有主见的人，年轻时敢于发表自己的见解。但在现实生活中，他却不得不一再委屈求全。从求学、求职，到为家庭和责任所束缚，他的人生始终被一只无形的手推着向前。

现在，终于退休了。他想摆脱这一切，走向大自然。

(2)

林教授的妻子两年前病逝。这段婚姻并非建立在爱情上，夫妻之间缺少思想深度的交流。可几十年里，两人为孩子和家庭相敬如宾，也算圆满。

年轻时，他也曾有过一段刻骨铭心的爱情。可作为独子，他必须承担 "传宗接代，孝敬长辈" 的责任，不得不接受父母安排的婚事。他的经历，仿佛与小说《家》中的大哥重叠：个人意志被家族与时代压下，心里的火焰，只能暗暗熄灭。

好在事业上，他小有成就，受到同事和社会的尊重。孩子也已成家立业，他的 "使命" 终于完成。于是，他告诉自己：一是时候走出圈子，活出想要的样子了。

(3)

然而，在他心底，始终有一段沉重的阴影。这阴影，来自他儿子的童年。第一个孩子是女儿。但是社会与家庭的声音却说： "女儿不算，林家还需要个儿子传宗接代"。

这是在独生子女政策最严厉的年代，再要孩子就是 "偷生" ，一旦被发现，就意味着丢掉工作、巨额罚款，甚至家庭的崩塌。他本人不想再要孩子，可妻子坚持，父母也施压。当妻子再次怀孕时，他犹豫了。可转念一想： 孩子是无辜的，堕胎太残忍了。于是，这个孩子被偷偷生下。

他们不敢给孩子上户口，只能托付给亲戚抚养。孩子不能叫 "爸爸、妈妈" ，只

能叫 "舅舅、舅妈"。在外人眼中，他是海外亲戚的孩子。直到七岁，爷爷奶奶托了无数关系，才终于为孩子办下户口，让他能回到父母身边上学。

可这段秘密，像一道伤痕，深深刻在孩子心里。长期的疏离让他变得敏感内向，从小背负着 "不敢承认亲生父母" 的痛苦。林教授对此愧疚至极，他从此把更多的心力放在儿子教育上，唯恐再欠他什么。幸好，儿子聪明懂事，举止有礼，后来考上理想的大学，也建立了自己的家庭和事业。

林教授心里反复对自己说：是时候放下了。

(4)

退休后，他开始走向自然。山川、河流、荒野，这些都成了他新的课堂。鸟鸣替代了喧嚣，风声冲淡了尘世的纷扰。走出圈子，不是抛弃过去，而是把过去放下。他要重新学会，只为自己而活。

可在宁静的旅途中，他常常在风声与树影间，听见往昔的回响。那些人、那些事，那些并肩而行、又在岁月中失散的朋友们。

他忽然明白：真正的 "出圈"，并不是逃离，而是有一天，他必须带着这些记忆与声音，重新回去继续生活。— 那才是归来。

Outside Opportunity's Gate

Prologue

The gate of opportunity - Sometimes fate needs only the gentlest push to keep a person forever on the wrong side of the threshold.

I · The Summer of 1977

Noon pressed like hot iron on the skin. Cicadas screamed in the locust trees. In the scent-down youth compound, drops fell from the laundry line and struck the dust forming tiny craters. A commune bicycle screeched at the gate. The young cadre swung off, briefcase thumping, his voice low but breathless:

"The college entrance exam has been restored!"

The words skipped across the yard like a stone on water—silence first, then widening ripples. A bowl nearly slipped. Someone gasped and clapped a hand over their mouth. Someone else squinted, muttering, "Don't let it be another rumor."

Li Jian stood in the doorway, thumb rubbing the cracked leather of his old accordion. The case was crazed like drought-split earth. Beyond the mud wall, the field ridges paled in the evening light. Heat rose in his chest—part joy, part trembling.

That night, a kerosene lamp wavered in a corner. He pulled out Math, Physics, Chemistry—pages rough with age, corners chewed thin. He sharpened pencil stubs to nubs and lined them up like a small brigade.

His roommate asked, "You really believe it?"

He smiled. "Believe it or not, I'll start studying."

"And if it falls through?"

"Then let it die in the books."

At dawn he went to the commune office—registration, subjects, medical exam, admission tickets. The cadre read as if crossing a minefield. Li Jian copied the essentials onto a scrap folded soft as cloth and pressed it into his pocket.

On the way back, sparrows hopped on the wires, the canal spilled light. His steps felt lighter. The road hadn't changed; his direction had. Class background had weighed on him like a stone, but if a door cracked even an inch, he would pour his whole life through.

He wrote three words on the first page of a notebook: Start from zero—and drove the strokes in like nails.

II · A Gifted Youth

That year he shot up and was placed in the top class. Sunlight slanted through the windows and seemed to halo his face. Sharp brows. An open smile. A casual, effortless grace.

On the court, he rose; the ball traced an arc and hissed the net. The yard erupted. In the auditorium, he shouldered his accordion; the first chord leapt, and the hall fell still as a held breath.

Teachers said, "He's too clever." essays came alive at the first stroke; the weekly bulletin was his domain.

But each time he filled the box for family class status, others wrote worker, poor peasant; he wrote, stiffly, child of Rightists. The teacher's eyes paused, a quiet sigh. Classmates' gazes cooled for a heartbeat—as if his radiance were only a mistake in the light.

At night, staring at the dark ceiling, a sentence pressed from within: If birth decides everything, what is the use of being bright?

He buried the line in his notebook: I must run faster than the shadows.

III · The Physical Exam

In the exam hall, the whisper of papers was like fine rain. Someone's knee jittered. He spread his sheet; the pen began to move, then flowed with quiet certainty. When he handed it in, a long-held weight inside him finally came to rest.

The results board went up. The crowd swelled. Names were read, and his came early. Applause, praise, envy, and the sourness that trails it—he could feel them on his back. That night he rolled in bed, seeing long tables in a library, sycamore shade, a classroom of voices, Saturday games. All of it felt a single threshold away.

The medical: corridors cold as glass, disinfectant in the nose. The doctor, eyes on the form, pressed his abdomen with a cool hand, and wrote quickly:

Enlarged liver.

He stalled; throat dry. "I'm well. I'm fully recovered. I can work. I can —study."

A glance. "Next."

The crowd pushed him out. The light swelled and dimmed like a tide. Those words glowed black in his mind.

Weeks later, the paper came: Rejected for health reasons. At night, his nails bit crescents into his palms. In the morning, someone joked, "Hey, college boy, why the long face?"

He laughed too loudly. "It's fine. A factory can be its own world."

When the laugh died, the light in his eyes was a blown-out match.

IV · The Factory and the Accordion

The machines roared like surf, day and night. Iron filings flashed under bare bulbs. Oil layered in the throat. His shoulders toughened under the blue uniform; calluses grew in the cups of his hands. After shift, cards clacked; he lit a cigarette and smiled once, thinly.

At night he set the accordion on his knees. The bulb burned dim; his shadow stretched long. The bellows opened and closed; the first note sighed and demanded at once. The tune at times knifed up as if to pierce the tin roof; at other times it sank like water traveling underground.

A bunkmate stirred, mumbling, "If he'd gone to college, he'd be someone. What a waste."

His knuckles blanched on the keys. One sentence haunted him: I should have been there.

Because of his excellent score, he was assigned to a newly established televised university. The admission note lit his eyes for a moment and then guttered out. A patch could not seal the tear.

Years later, at an ultrasound, the doctor said mildly, "Everything's normal."

He stepped out of the hospital gate and heard a door inside him slam shut again, iron against iron.

V · The City and the Tracks

Because of his good performance in the countryside, Li Jian was recruited by a county machinery factory. Not long after, his parents were finally cleared of their "Rightist" labels and returned to the big city they had once been forced to leave.

When the news reached him, he stood in shock for a long time. The stone on his chest seemed to lighten—at last, the hope of reunion. For a moment, he even dared to imagine: if he could return to his parents' side, perhaps his life could start anew.

But reality once again stretched out its cold hand. To transfer to his parents' city, he had to give up his relatively stable job at the factory and accept a harsher post—railway track inspector.

He did not hesitate. "No matter how hard it is, if I can be with them, it's worth it," he told himself. Yet in his heart, there was a faint bitterness. Others, once their families were rehabilitated, found better jobs and brighter prospects. He had the railroad and the wind. But he hid the disappointment, telling his parents only: "Once I'm back, there'll be chances to change later."

It was a job that pitted man against nature. In summer, the rails burned hot under the sun, like fiery snakes. He walked them kilometer by kilometer, hammering, listening. Sweat dripped on the steel and vanished in white steam. Duting winter nights, the north wind drove snow into his face. Wrapped in a thick coat, his shadow stretched long as he walked alone along endless tracks. The howl of the wind often tricked him into thinking a train was about to burst out of the darkness.

More than once, he thought about giving up. At night, a voice whispered: If I had gone to college, what would life be now? Sitting in a bright classroom? Writing a thesis? Reading in a library? Then he would take a hard drag on his cigarette, swallow the bitterness, and remind himself: morning would come, and he still had to walk the rails.

At home, his parents asked eagerly about his work. He smiled and said, "It's fine, not too hard." But when he turned away to light a cigarette, his hand trembled. That quiet endurance was his last shield for them.

By day, he was a silent worker. Colleagues complained of low pay and heavy labor; he kept his head down, smoking. The smoke blurred his eyes and hid the weight in his heart. At night, he still picked up his accordion, but the music no longer soared. It came out slow and heavy, like a weary breath of someone too tired to dream.

In this city, he finally shared the same sky with his aging parents. But he knew that the sky that should have been his own had already collapsed.

VI · Ending and Remembrance

Many years later, while traveling alone, Professor Lin often thought of his old friend.

When the wind swept across the wilderness, he seemed to see that spirited boy again— standing tall on the basketball court, smiling brightly, eyes full of light. As if nothing unfortunate had ever happened. Yet in the blink of an eye, the figure blurred, leaving only a lone back, walking along endless tracks.

He remembered that smile—so open, so contagious. But after blow upon blow from fate, it grew dimmer. Years of smoking had stained his teeth yellow and black, his face etched with early weariness. It was hard to find in him, the handsome youth once admired like a star by classmates.

Sometimes, Professor Lin recalled a line his friend had written: — "I must run faster than the shadows." Back then, he had laughed and said, "What a thing to write." But now the words pierced like needles. His friend had run all his life, yet the shadow of fate had always been faster.

Such is life. It was not a lack of talent, nor of strength, but of timing. At the most crucial moment, fate slammed shut a door, locking away his future. People sighed: "If only he had gone to college, he would have achieved great things. What a pity." But such words were nothing more than whispers in the wind.

Professor Lin had walked through countless cities, seen countless sights. Yet in the silence of night, when the wind howled, he could almost hear it again—that heavy, lingering sound of the accordion.

In that music were defiance, struggle, and a final resistance against destiny. He knew— Some people are not born without wings. It's just that their wings were broken before they could ever fly.

机会的门外

引子

机会的门外 —
命运只需轻轻一推，就能把人挡在门槛之外。

1 · 1977年的夏天

70年代末的中国，是一个既令人激动又令人感慨的年代。四人帮倒台，十年动乱终结，国家迫切需要一条新路，让亿万人重新看到希望。

1977年的夏天，风仿佛忽然学会了说话。

离县城不远的知青院里，晾衣绳绷得笔直，湿衫滴水。烈日炙烤，大地生烟。忽然，一辆公社的自行车嘎吱停下，车把上挂着公文包的青年跳下车，高声宣布："恢复高考的通知下来了！"

话音如石子落水，院子炸开。有人碗差点掉地，有人惊呼捂嘴，也有人眯眼嘟囔："又是风声吧？"十年了，大学靠关系和名额，如今一句"恢复"，能让时间倒回去？

傍晚，天边燃起一片桃色的云。汽油灯点亮，有人翻出鼠咬过的旧课本，有人仰望星空，眼睛亮得像刚出水。也有人沉默坐在台阶，指甲缝里满是泥土。

李建靠在门框上，手指摩挲着旧手风琴。琴箱裂纹如旱地龟裂。他望见田埂在余晖中泛白，胸口忽然涌起热流，像有人在里面点燃了火。

他想起远在边疆的父亲、在农场劳作的母亲——他们受过高等教育，却因直言被打成右派，从城市流放。他自己，高中毕业未满十七岁，就被下放农村，本以为一生归宿只是个普通工人。

如今，"恢复高考"四个字，像一道光劈开厚石。

——也许，命运终于要松口了？

夜深，煤油灯摇曳。桌上摊着《数学》《物理》《化学》。那些年课堂不是口号，就是农机养猪，他几乎没学到真正的知识。但他仍热爱数理，靠自学硬撑。

"你真信？"同屋的伙伴问。

他笑答："信不信，先学起来。"

"要是黄了呢？"

"那就让它黄在书上。"

次日清晨，他与队友去公社打听：报名、科目、体检、准考证。干部翻文件，语气谨慎。他把每一条都记在折得起皱的纸片上，按进兜里。

回程时，河水闪光，麻雀跳跃。他脚步忽然轻快——不是路好走，而是心里终于有了去处。

2 · 少年才华

他曾是学校里最耀眼的少年。

那年开学，他骤然抽高，被分进一班。阳光斜照进教室，他的脸庞仿佛自带光晕。眉目分明，笑容开阔，举手投足潇洒。女同学忍不住偷看，男同学心里暗暗嫉妒。

篮球场上，他的跳跃像电影定格，球入网，全场沸腾。文艺汇演时，他拉起手风琴，琴声回荡，连最顽皮的学生都安静下来。

老师们说："这孩子聪明得过分。"

课程一通百通，作业轻松满分，作文生动感人。板报由他绘制，每周更新。才智、运动、艺术，他一样不缺，像是命运的宠儿。

他自己也清楚，于是笑得更自信，步子更轻快，像展翅的小鹰。灰色年代里，他是少数几个自带光亮的人。

但光亮背后，总有阴影。

填写 "家庭成分" 时，别人写 "工人" "贫下中农"，他却只能写下 "右派子女"。老师沉默，同学的目光冷下来，仿佛刚才的一切光芒只是幻觉。

表面上，他依旧大笑。夜里，他却盯着天花板：

——如果出身决定一切，我再聪明又有什么用？

孤独的夜，他在本子上写下一行字：

——"我要跑得比阴影更快。"

3 · 考试与体检

考试那天，考场挤满十年积压的希望。很多考生比他大一轮。人人都在拼命。

他准备充分，屡屡提前交卷。成绩公布时，他名列前茅。那几天，他走在路上能感到目光追随 — 羡慕、惊叹、嫉妒。

夜里，他想象大学的图书馆、梧桐树、讲台与篮球场。未来近得像伸手可及。

录取表格上 "健康情况" 一栏，他犹豫片刻，还是写下："曾患 A 型肝炎。"心中微颤，却安慰自己——早已痊愈。

体检那天，消毒水刺鼻，白炽灯冷冷垂下。医生冰凉的手指在他腹部按了几下，潦草写下：

— "肝脏偏大，不正常"

那几个字像铁锤钉在他心口。"我已经痊愈了！" 他急声辩解。

医生冷冷抬眼："下一个。"

几周后，通知下来：因身体健康原因，未被录取。

那一夜，他手指掐出血印。第二天，队友打趣："哎呀，大学生，咋拉脸子？"

他笑得灿烂："没事，去工厂也能闯出天地！"

笑容落下，眼神却暗了。

就在那段日子，他和同队的一位姑娘走得很近。她清秀动人，笑中带光。复习时，她常坐在他身边听题，笔记上工整写下每一步。

成绩公布后，她鼓起勇气表白："不管咱们在哪读书，都要继续努力。将来我们一起生活，好不好？"

他悸动不已，那是他从未敢奢望的温柔。

可现实很快撕开幻梦。他因体检落榜，而她考上外地中专。临行前的傍晚，槐树下，她紧紧握着他的手：

"你要坚持，等我毕业，我们就一起走下去。"

他将这句话刻进心里。

然而，不到一年，一切就变了。在机械厂做工的他，收到她的来信。字迹娟秀，却冷硬：父母不同意，要求她断绝关系。

那晚，他独自拉起手风琴。琴声颤抖，像风里将熄的火苗。从此，他再没提起过这段爱情。

4 · 工厂与手风琴

爱情破碎，命运封门。生活却还要继续。

工厂轰鸣，机油与铁屑弥漫。他穿着蓝色工装，肩膀磨硬，双手生茧。白天沉默劳作，夜晚独坐铁床，抱起旧手风琴。

昏黄灯下，风箱缓缓张开，第一声低沉的音符像叹息，又像追问。旋律里有光亮，也有疼痛；有时急促，仿佛要冲破铁皮屋顶；有时低沉，像在地底缓缓流淌。

偶尔，工友惊醒，叹气："这孩子要是能去大学读书，准能成才。可惜啊。"

他听见，却只是拉得更紧，指节发白。

一我本该在那里，我也该有另一种人生！

电大录取通知书一度点亮过他的眼睛，很快又熄灭。他知道，那只是补丁，无法真正愈合青春的裂口。

多年后，B超结果显示：肝脏一切正常。那一刻，他仿佛听见青春的门再次被重重关上。

白日，他是沉默工人；夜晚，他用琴声赎回自己。在别人眼里，他只是工人。可胸口仍燃烧着一段旋律——属于梦想的火焰，却无人能听见。

5 · 回城与路检工人

父母终于平反，回到大城市。他也调回去，但必须放弃机械厂的岗位，去做铁路路检工。

"哪怕再苦，只要能在他们身边，就值了。" 他告诉自己。

盛夏，铁轨滚烫，他一公里一公里走下去，汗水滴在铁轨上，瞬间蒸发成白印。

寒冬，北风裹挟雪沙，他缩紧棉衣，孤独走在无边铁道上，耳边呼啸让他恍惚下一秒就有火车冲出黑暗。

夜深时，他常想：

如果当年进了大学，如今的自己会怎样？是不是正坐在教室里写论文？

他狠狠吸一口烟，把酸涩压下去。因为天亮后，他还要继续走在铁轨上。

父母总关切询问，他只笑着说："挺好，不累。"

可转过身，点烟时，手却微微颤抖。白天，他沉默劳作；夜晚，他仍抱起手风琴。可琴声已不再昂扬，只剩下低沉的喘息。旋律里裹着风霜与孤独，像一条暗河，淹没了他未竟的青春。

6 · 结局与追忆

多年以后，林教授独自旅行，常常想起这位少年好友。风吹过荒野，他仿佛又看见那个意气风发的少年：挺拔站在篮球场，笑容明亮，眼睛里闪着光。可眨眼间，身影模糊，只剩背影，在漫长铁轨上孤独前行。

他记得，那笑容曾感染所有人，却在命运一次次打击下渐渐暗淡。多年烟火，把少年的俊朗磨成疲惫。再难看见，当初那个自带光亮的少年。

他想起好友写下的一句话：

——"我要跑得比阴影更快。"

当年，他笑着说："这小子真会写。"如今想起，却像针扎般疼。他明白，好友奔跑了一生，可命运的阴影始终快一步。不是没有才华，不是没有力量，而是生不逢时。命运在最关键的一刻，关上了那扇门，把他挡在机会之外。

有人叹息："这孩子要是能上大学，准能成才。可惜啊。"

可这些话，也只是风中的回声。

林教授走过无数城市，看过无数风景。夜深风起，他仿佛听见，那段压抑而悠长的手风琴声仍在回荡。那琴声里，有不甘，有挣扎，有对命运最后的抵抗。

他也终于明白：有些人，不是没有翅膀，而是被挡在机会的门外。那扇门一旦关上，就再也没有打开过。

The Sorrow of Love

Prologue

In that turbulent era, love was never just between two people. It was a fate entangled and torn apart by the weight of its time.

1. The First Encounter

The medical school library always smelled faintly of ink and paper. Outside, shadows of locust trees dappled the desks, and the air carried the cool stillness of early summer.

Liu Di pushed open the heavy wooden door, clutching her thick biochemistry textbook. At just eighteen, she was a second-year medical student. Raised in a family of veteran military cadres, she had received a careful upbringing. Intelligent yet shy, delicate and refined, she carried a purity reminiscent of Lin Daiyu from the classics. She loved her books, cherished learning, and longed for a deeper kind of intellectual resonance.

That day, she saw Fang Ming for the first time. Fang Ming was thirty, among the first cohort of graduate students after the reinstatement of college entrance exams. His family background was complicated, and during the Cultural Revolution he had been sent to teach at a middle school before finally entering graduate studies. He had entered a "politically correct" marriage with a factory worker—a so-called "revolutionary wife"—to safeguard his future and fulfill the duty of carrying on the family line. But in that marriage, there was no true love, only obligation and restraint.

In the library that day, he sat by the window. His white shirt sleeves were casually rolled, an English journal open before him, his pen moving steadily across his notebook. The sunlight framed his sharp features, his eyes intent and steady, carrying the quiet confidence of a man seasoned by years.

Liu Di's heart trembled. She did not ask who he was, nor did she wonder if he already had a family. She only realized in that instant that a single presence could make the entire world fade away.

Later, in lab sessions, their paths crossed more often. Fang Ming explained procedures with a voice that was low and precise, his gestures carrying the ease of maturity. At the dining table he was refined and witty, his manners impeccable. To Liu Di, so young and just entering society, such seasoned charm was irresistibly magnetic.

Her intelligence and purity, in turn, deeply moved Fang Ming. In her attentive gaze, he seemed to rediscover the light of youth and ideals. Drawn irresistibly to one another, their feelings burned quietly, inevitably.

2. The Storm

Rumors spread quickly and soon reached Fang Ming's wife. She stormed into the campus, weeping and shouting, hurling vile accusations that shredded Liu Di's dignity. The spectacle resembled the farcical aftermath of the Cultural Revolution—loud, chaotic, and without a shred of grace. Of course she refused to divorce; she would never let those two despicable people have the satisfaction of being together.

The Party branch convened a criticism meeting. Teachers and students were ordered to take sides, and the atmosphere was stifling and merciless.

Fang Ming did not shrink back. When pressed by hostile voices, his eyes shone steady as he declared coldly:

"I have done nothing wrong. To follow love, to seek happiness—these are never crimes."

His words dropped like a stone into still water. For a moment the hall was silent, then erupted in even harsher condemnation. Some called him corrupt; others branded him a traitor to morality. Newspapers soon carried editorials, holding him up as a "negative example" to warn the masses.

Liu Di was thrust into the eye of the storm. Barely eighteen, she should have been enjoying her studies and her youth. Instead, she endured fear and humiliation, forced to bear the scrutiny of all. Many classmates pitied her, but no one dared to speak up. It was an age of "drawing clear lines from mistakes"—everyone feared being implicated.

3. The Cost of Love

For his "stubborn attitude," Fang Ming was expelled from the medical school and sent back to his old middle school. But the classroom podium had denied him; he was assigned only menial chores. From a spirited young teacher, he became a marginal figure at the school.

Though Liu Di completed her five years of study, the scandal left her without a diploma. She was sent instead to a factory clinic in her hometown. By day, she measured temperatures and wrote prescriptions for workers. By night, she sat alone under a dim lamp, gazing at letters from her former classmates, lost in thought.

She could have gone much further. With her intelligence, her gentleness, her drive, she might have built a future in medicine. But this love had cut her path short, brutally and without mercy.

4. Remembrance

Years later, Professor Lin passed that same middle school alone. The old classrooms were gone, replaced by a gleaming three-story building.

He froze, struck still. It was as if time had reversed: he saw Fang Ming at the podium again, white shirt crisp, chalk carving clean arcs across the board; and in the front row, a girl who looked uncannily like Liu Di, her eyes bright as morning light, fixed upon him.

For a fleeting moment, youth seemed to live again. But when the vision faded, only the new building and unfamiliar faces of a younger generation remained. A pang of sorrow struck his heart. He understood then—this was not only the sorrow of Fang Ming and Liu Di, but the sorrow of an entire generation.

At that time, love was never a free choice. It was a fate torn apart by politics and fear.

《爱情的悲哀》

序幕

在那个动荡的年代，爱情不是两个人的事，而是被时代裹挟的命运。

1· 初遇

医学院的图书馆，总带着淡淡的墨香与纸张的味道。窗外的槐树影子斑驳，映在书桌上，空气里透着初夏的清凉。

刘迪抱着厚厚的《生物化学》，推开沉重的木门。她刚满十八岁，是二年级的医学生。生长在军队老干部家庭，自幼接受良好教育。她聪慧腼腆，气质清秀纤弱，眉眼间带着几分林黛玉式的纯净。她热爱书本，对知识有一种天然的渴望与上进心。

那一天，她第一次见到了方明。

方明三十几岁，是恢复高考后首批研究生之一。因为家庭出身复杂，文革中大学毕业被迫分配到中学教书，后才得以考取研究生。他有过一段政治"正确"的婚姻，妻子是工人，在文革动乱时代这种革命婚姻是稳定前途和"传宗接代"一种改良办法。然而这段婚姻里没有真正的爱情，更多是责任与束缚。

在图书馆的那一刻，他正坐在靠窗的位置。白衬衫的袖口随意挽起，桌上摊着一本英文期刊，笔尖不断划过笔记本。阳光照在他侧脸，轮廓分明，眼神专注，透着一种成熟男子的沉稳与自信。

刘迪怦然心动。

她没有去想他是谁，更没有去问他是否已有家庭。她只是突然明白，一个人光是坐在那里，就能让世界黯淡下去。

后来，在实验课上，两人有了更多接触。方明讲解实验步骤时，声音低沉而清晰，举手投足间带着成熟与风度。他在餐桌上也格外讲究，谈吐风趣，气质儒雅。对初入社会的刘迪来说，这种成熟的魅力带着致命吸引。

而刘迪的聪慧与纯净，也深深打动了方明。在她专注的目光里，他仿佛重新看见了青春与理想的光。两人互相吸引，情感在不知不觉间燃烧。

2· 风暴

谣言很快传开，传到方明妻子的耳里。她在校园里嚎哭打闹，满嘴污言，把刘迪的人格践踏得一无所有。场面像极了文革余波的闹剧，毫无尊严。当然她坚决拒绝离婚，她绝不会让那两个可鄙的人得偿所愿，走向一起。

学校党支部召开批判会。师生们被要求表态，气氛压抑而残酷。

在这种情况下，方明没有退缩。他声音冷冷，但眼神坚定："我没有错。追求爱情，寻找幸福，从来不是罪。再说我们也没有做任何过分的事情。"

一石激起千层浪。会场一度寂然，随即爆发出更猛烈的指责。有人骂他腐化堕落，有人斥他大逆不道。当地报纸甚至撰写一篇社论指名道姓把他们塑造成"反面教材"，警示所有的人。

刘迪被推上舆论的风口浪尖。她才十八岁，本应享受学习与青春，却在恐惧与羞辱中被迫承受一切。虽然大多数同学心里同情，却无人敢替他们辩护。那是一个"与错误划清界限"的年代，每个人都怕被牵连。

3 · 爱情的代价

方明因态度"顽固"被医学院开除，只能回到原中学。可学校再也没有给他讲台的机会，只让他做些零碎杂务。从年轻意气的教师，沦为校园的边缘人，杂务工。

刘迪虽完成了五年学业，却因这段丑闻未获毕业证书，只能被分配到家乡的工厂医务所。白天，她为工人量体温、写处方；夜晚，她独坐在昏黄的灯下，翻看昔日同学的来信，神情恍惚。

她本可以走得更远。聪慧腼腆、追求进取，她原本有机会在医学上有所建树。但这一段爱情，把她的未来生生掐断。

4 · 回忆

多年后，林教授独自路过那所中学。旧教学楼早已被推倒，取而代之的是一幢崭新的三层大楼。

他忽然怔住了。仿佛时光倒流，他似乎看见当年讲台上的方老师，白衬衫整洁，粉笔划出清晰的弧线；似乎课堂第一排坐着一位酷似刘迪的女孩，眼神专注，澄澈如晨曦。

一切仿佛停留在青春的岁月。可当幻影消散，眼前只剩陌生的楼宇与新一代学生的面孔。林教授心头一酸。他明白，这不仅是方明与刘迪的悲哀，更是一代人的悲哀。

在那个年代，爱情从来不是自由的选择，而是被制度、舆论与恐惧撕裂的命运。

Returning

In the second year of his retirement, Professor Lin traveled widely—from the water towns of the South to the barren plains of the North. Rivers, winds, and mountain shadows outside the train window often made him feel as if he had stepped beyond that suffocating circle and was finally moving toward freedom.

But he soon realized: true freedom was not found on the road.

In a noisy market, he saw a boy carrying an old accordion. His heart tightened, as though Li Jian's trembling chords still echoed music once played to resist fate amid the roar of machines.

In the corridor of a train, hearing students discuss studying abroad and their bright futures, he remembered Fang Ming. He could still picture the classroom of years past: chalk tracing clean arcs across the blackboard, eyes shining with light. Yet that light, over time, had been steadily extinguished.

On a winter night, passing a hospital under harsh white lights, he thought of Liu Di—the gentle, gifted student who might have gone far in medicine, but whose path was broken by rumor and by a love never meant to be.

These names and fates had never left him. He understood now: none of them were distant stories, but living echoes, woven into his own life. And yet, the road ahead still stretched open.

In mountains and rivers, in windswept fields and wide skies, he felt—for the first time—the vastness of life itself. Freedom did not escape but carrying these memories forward. Li Jian, Fang Ming, Liu Di, and countless silent companions—their unfinished youth, broken careers, and extinguished loves—had all become part of him.

They were his true luggage. On the day of his return, he stood at his window, watching the city sink into night. Streetlamps flickered on, one by one, like memories rising from the dark. Softly, he whispered:

"I have not forgotten you."

A few days later, he went alone to a river outside the city. The winter snow had just melted; the water murmured, clear and cold. He bent to pick up a stone and tossed it into the current. Ripples spread outward—circle upon circle—like his own life, layered yet unbroken.

He closed his eyes, letting the wind move through bare branches. In the whispers of the air, he seemed to hear again the vanished sounds:

the accordion's melody, the scratch of chalk on a blackboard, the rustle of turning pages, the soft voice of a child calling "Papa."

These voices had never truly left. And suddenly, he smiled—not a smile of release, but of understanding. To step out was never to abandon, but to carry their shadows forward— toward a farther horizon, toward a deeper return.

As the night deepened, the river glowed pale beneath the moon. He turned back slowly, the hollowness in his chest gone at last. He had finally learned: freedom was not solitude. It was reconciliation with memory, and the courage to walk on.

归来

　　林教授退休后的第二年，他走遍了南方的水乡与北方的草原。车窗外的河流、风声、山影，让他一度以为自己正走出那个压抑的圈子，奔向自由。

　　可他渐渐明白，真正的自由也许并不只在路途上。在集市的喧嚣里，他看见一个抱着旧手风琴的少年，心口忽然一酸——仿佛又听见李建的琴声，那颤抖的和弦曾在工厂轰鸣里，与命运抗争。

　　在火车的走廊，他听见年轻学生们谈论出国留学与未来，便想起了方明。当年的课堂上，方老师充满了自信，声音洪亮而清晰，眼神闪烁着光。可那光，最终被现实一点点熄灭。

　　在冬夜的医院外，白炽灯也让他心头一紧。他想起了刘迪，那位聪慧温婉的女大学生，她本可以走得更远，却在流言与爱情的裹挟中跌落。

这些名字，这些命运，从未远离。他明白，他们的青春与希望，被时代生生截断，而自己也不过是同一场风暴中的一员而已。

可是，往前走的路还在。山川河流，荒野天空，让他第一次感受到生命本身的辽阔。自由，不是逃离，而是带着这些记忆继续前行。李建、方明、刘迪，还有那些沉默的朋友们，他们未竟的梦想，已融入他的人生。他们，才是他真正的行装。

归来的一天，他站在窗前，看着夜色中的城市。街灯一盏盏亮起，仿佛无数记忆在黑暗里浮现。他轻声自语："我没有忘记你们。"

几天后，他又独自去了郊外的河边。冬雪刚融，水声潺潺，空气清冷澄澈。他拾起一块石子，抛向河心。涟漪层层荡开，像他的人生，一圈又一圈，终将融入大河的流动。

他闭上眼，耳畔似乎响起逝去的声音：手风琴的旋律，黑板上的粉笔声，图书馆翻页的沙沙声，孩子轻轻唤 "爸爸" 的声音……

这些声音，从未远离。他忽然笑了。不是解脱的笑，而是释怀的笑。归来，也许不只是回到某个既定的地方，而是回到记忆深处，然后带着记忆，走向新的生活。

夜色渐深，河水在月光下泛白。他缓缓转身，心中已不再空洞。他终于明白：自由，并不是孤身一人的存在，而是与过往和解，并勇敢地向前。

Afterword

These stories were born from memory of a generation during a special time. They are not merely personal recollections, but fragments of a shared past—echoes of youth lost to duty, voices stifled by fear, loves fractured by history.

If there is one hope in sharing this collection, it is that readers may glimpse not only the weight of the past, but also the quiet strength within it. Because even in silence, memory endures.

And through memory, we return—again and again—to what it means to live, to love, to be free.

— Snow Ray

《后记》

这些故事诞生于一代人的真实生活之中。它们不仅是个人的回忆，更是过去共同的片段 — 青春在政治运动中失落，声音在恐惧中被压抑，爱情在历史里被撕裂。

写下它们，是直面悲伤，也是触碰温情．若这本小说集能带给读者一些启示，那便是：过去的痛伤固然存在，但其中也蕴藏着生命静默的力量。因为记忆不会消散。而正是通过记忆，我们一次次归来，找回生命的本质，找回爱的意义，找回自由的灵魂。

— 瑞雪

About the Author

Snow Ray is the pen name of a physician-scientist and writer whose work bridges history, memory, and resilience. Through fiction, she gives voice to stories of love, silence, and survival, weaving intimate lives into the broader currents of history.